Brad
The Wonder Baby

by Dianne Bates

illustrated by Luke Jurevicius

STANLEY
THORNES

The Characters

Brad Crumble
did not like being born.

Sophie Crumble
had a big secret.

Mum and Dad Crumble

The Setting

CONTENTS

CHAPTER

Brad Meets His Family

Brad Crumble did not like being born. A doctor slapped his bottom. Someone fiddled with his belly button. Bright lights hurt his eyes.

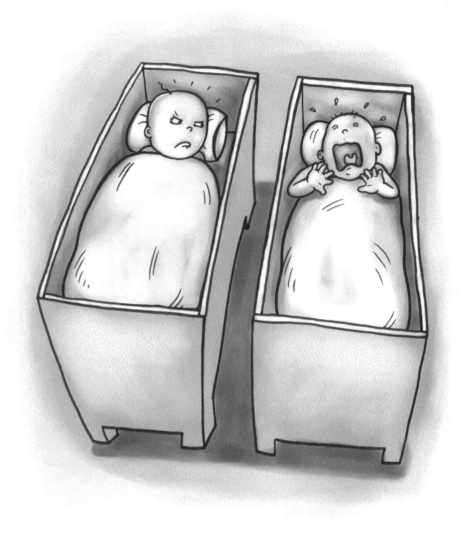

Brad did not like the hospital. The other babies slept or cried. No-one wanted to talk or play. He was bored.

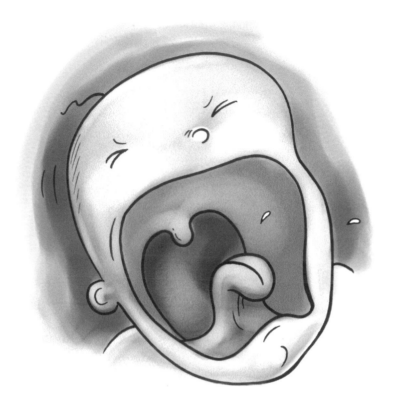

Mum and Dad were no fun.
"Goo," said Dad.

"Gah," said Mum.
"Kitchy, kitchy, koo."

Brad yelled at them to speak English.
His parents only heard, "Waaaaaah".

"He's got a good set of lungs," said his dad.

"He's hungry," said his mum.

"He's cute," said his sister, Sophie.

Brad Can Fly

On Brad's first night at home he threw off his blanket.
"Right!" he said, flapping his arms.
"Now for some fun."

He flew up to the ceiling. *Zap!* Just like that.
"I didn't know I could do that," he said.
He looked down at his room.

Brad flapped his arms again. Down he zoomed. *Zoom!* Just like that. "What fun," Brad thought.

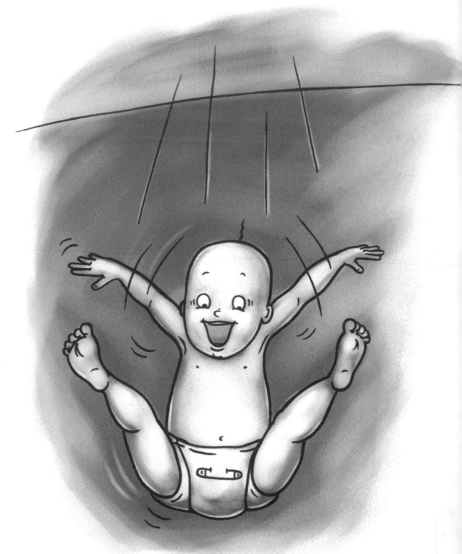

He flapped again and up he flew.
He flipped
      and dipped.
He whizzed
      and whirled.
He twisted
      and curled.

Up to the ceiling, down to the floor,
across to the wall he flew.
"Yippee!" he cried.

Oh no! Footsteps! Someone was
walking down the hall. Brad flew back
into his cot. He dived under his
blanket and closed his eyes.

The door opened.
"Baby's asleep," Dad thought.
He yawned and went back down the
hall to bed.

Brad waited. After a while he heard
"ZZZZZZZZZZZZZZZZ."
Dad was snoring.
"zzzzzzzzzzzzzzzzz."
So was Mum.

"ZZZZZZZZZZ."
So was his sister Sophie.

"They're all asleep. Now I can explore,"
thought Brad.

CHAPTER 3

Brad Flies Outside

Brad flew round and round. He made circles in the air. He got dizzy and threw up half his dinner.

Then Brad flew out of his room. He was off to explore the house.

It was dark. Brad couldn't see much. He didn't know how to turn on the lights.

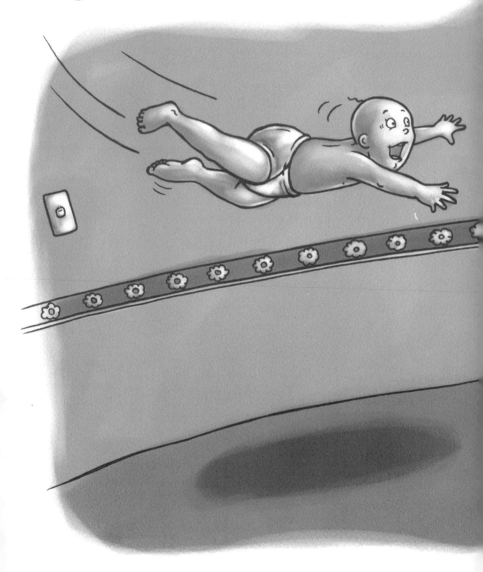

Brad could see light coming in through the windows. He could see houses, trees and cars through the window.

Brad wanted to go outside. The living room window was open.

Swish went the curtains as Brad flew past them.

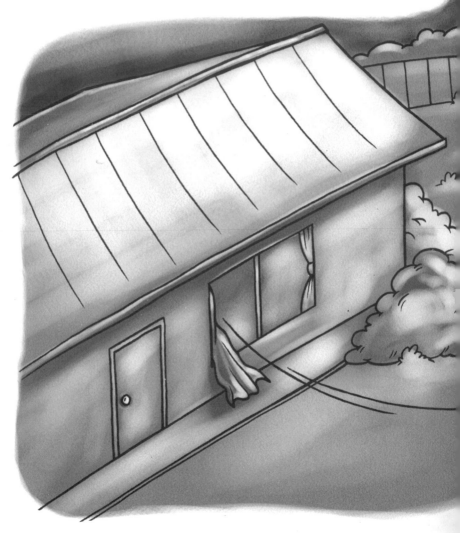

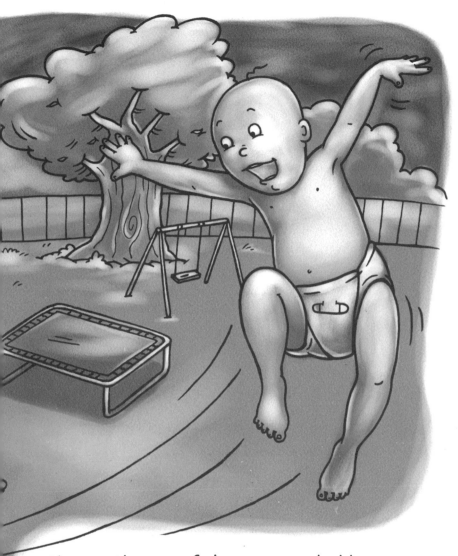

Above the roof he zoomed. He was
so high! By the light of the moon
he could see the garden. It had a
swing, a sandpit and a trampoline.

Brad flew down to find out what each thing did. He tried to land on the trampoline. He bounced into the air. "Wheeee!" squealed Brad.

He bounced again.
He flipped
    and dipped.
He twisted
    and curled.
Brad giggled and squealed.

CHAPTER 4

Brad Almost Gets Caught

When the person next door opened the back door, Brad whizzed up into a tall tree. He didn't want anyone to know he could fly.

He sat on a branch and watched.
The man stood at his back door. He
looked into the darkness. He shone a
torch into the darkness.

The torch light dazzled Brad's eyes.
Oh no! The man would see him! The
man walked into the garden. Closer
and closer the man came.

"Is there anyone out there, Bill?" a woman's voice called from inside the house.

"There's no one out here, Dear," the man said. He went back inside.

Then Brad saw the scariest thing.
Two eyes were floating in the air
above him.

Brad's heart beat hard in his chest.
He made a mess in his nappy.

Brad screamed. He fell off the branch.
Down he fell,
       down,
          down,
             down.

Brad was just about to hit the ground
when he remembered he could fly. He
flapped his arms and flew up.

He flew up to another tree. He had to zoom away from the scary eyes that said, "Hoot! Hoot!"

CHAPTER 5

Brad Meets a Monster

Brad should have gone home but he was having fun. He flew onto a nearby roof. He looked down the chimney. He slid down the roof tiles.

Brad looked down into this new garden.
Near the back fence was a little house.
Brad flew down to take a closer look.

The house was dark and smelly.
Something was asleep inside. Brad
reached out and touched its nose. The
thing with a cold wet nose woke up.
"Grrr…"

Brad flew away as fast as he could.
"Woof! Woof!"
The barks were getting louder and
louder.
"Woof! Woof!"

A light went on in Brad's house. "O-oh!" thought Brad. "I'd better get back before Mum and Dad get up."

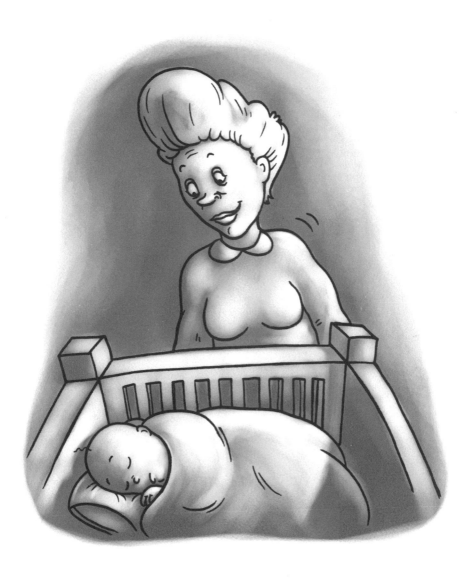

Brad flew back to his room. When his mum looked in on him Brad was fast asleep.

CHAPTER 6

Brad and Sophie

Brad loved his sister, Sophie. She spent lots of time with him. She talked to him. She didn't say "goo goo" or "kitchy kitchy koo".

Sophie told him stories and sang songs to him. She patted him on the back when he had a pain in his belly. She stroked Brad's head when he couldn't sleep.

"I have a really big secret," Sophie whispered in Brad's ear. "No one in the whole world knows my secret. Maybe one day I will tell you."

Brad wanted to tell Sophie *his* secret. Sophie seemed to be just the right person, but Brad wasn't sure yet.

One day Brad saw a torch on top of the fridge. That night Brad flew into the kitchen and picked up the torch.

He took the torch with him on his trip to the park. He shone the torch on everything he saw. He looked inside shop windows. He woke up sleeping dogs.

On this trip, some people saw Brad!

CHAPTER

Brad's Secret Is Discovered

"I've seen a flying saucer," a man told the police.

"I must be seeing things," said a little old lady. "I'll have to get my eyes tested."

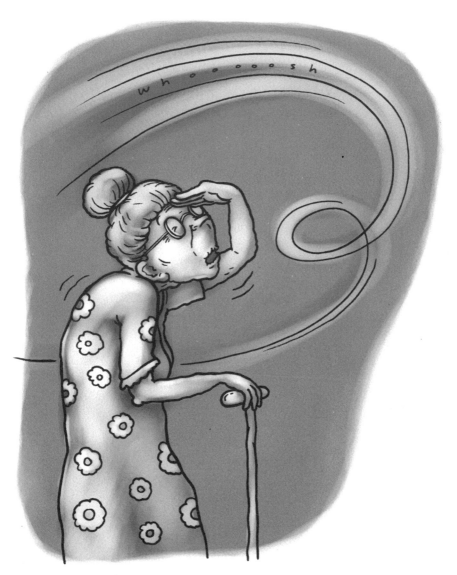

A man lying in the park saw Brad. "A flying baby with a torch," he muttered. He put down his bottle of beer.

Brad flew back home. He was about to go in through the window when he saw someone inside. They had a torch too!

"Oh, no!" thought Brad. "What will I do?"

Brad pressed his face against the window to see who it was. He couldn't see at first. Was it Mum? Was it Dad? Maybe it was a stranger. A burglar? Brad was scared.

The torch was moving. It was going up and up. It went higher until it was almost at the ceiling!

Brad was so surprised that he knocked his torch against the window.

The torch beam flashed onto Brad.
The light blinded him. He had been
seen!

"Brad!" It was sister Sophie.
The torch she was holding dropped to
the floor.
Brad was so happy to see Sophie
that he flew right into her arms.

"You can fly!" Sophie sounded amazed. "This is *the* most incredible thing in the world!"

Now Brad knew Sophie's big secret.
She could fly too.

"I thought I was the only person in the world who could fly," whispered Sophie. "But you can fly too! Brad, we are going to have such fun!"

From then on the two of them went flying together. They had great fun but they never told anyone their secret.

No one, to this day, knows Brad and Sophie's secret!
(Except for you.)

GLOSSARY

amazed
very surprised

ceiling
the top of a room —
opposite the floor

chimney
where the smoke escapes
from a fireplace

dizzy
when your head spins

explore
to look around a new place

flying saucer
a spaceship shaped
like a saucer

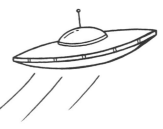

snore
a loud noise made by someone
who is sleeping

torch
a light you can carry

whirled
tumbled around and around

whizzed
moved in a big rush

Di Bates

What is your favourite breakfast?

Freshly squeezed orange juice, croissants, scrambled egg and bacon.

Who is your favourite cartoon character?

Calvin, of Calvin and Hobbs.

What was your least favourite activity at school?

Folk dancing.

Why is the sky blue?

Because that's the best colour to form a background for the birds of the world.

Luke Jurevicius

What is your favourite breakfast?

If I had my way ... chocolate pudding.

Who is your favourite cartoon character?

Mr Magoo.

What was your least favourite activity at school?

Waiting in line at the canteen.

Why is the sky blue?

Because all the colours had a vote and blue won.